T0380480

THE LEGEND OF THE ORBS

TEMPERANCE

Open your eyes to the vision...

MUDIWA ADRIAN DORO

AuthorHouse™ UK
1663 Liberty Drive
Bloomington, IN 47403 USA
www.authorhouse.co.uk
Phone: 0800 047 8203 (Domestic TFN)
+44 1908 723714 (International)

© 2019 Mudiwa Adrian Doro. All rights reserved.

No part of this book may be reproduced, stored
in a retrieval system, or transmitted by any means
without the written permission of the author.

Published by AuthorHouse 09/10/2019

ISBN: 978-1-7283-9204-2 (sc)
ISBN: 978-1-7283-9203-5 (e)

Print information available on the last page.

Any people depicted in stock imagery provided by Getty Images are models,
and such images are being used for illustrative purposes only.
Certain stock imagery © Getty Images.

This book is printed on acid-free paper.

Because of the dynamic nature of the Internet, any web addresses or links contained in
this book may have changed since publication and may no longer be valid. The views
expressed in this work are solely those of the author and do not necessarily reflect the
views of the publisher, and the publisher hereby disclaims any responsibility for them.

authorHOUSE®

THE LEGEND OF THE ORBS SEMBLANCE

Chapter 1
DREAMING

· · · · · · · · · · · · · ·

Echoes, voices, shapes. The same dream over and over again, all in a void of darkness that only I could locate. Unknown echoes followed by bizarre voices, the dream always ended the same way, with me being swallowed by the non-certain shape. I was trapped in that shape forever.

My feet touched the stone-cold mahogany floorboards. They whined under my weight as I slipped on my feet-eating crocodile slippers. I dragged my half-asleep body to the kitchen, after the dream I always felt thirsty.

Rudolph, the family cat, woke up purring, its green eyes shining in the darkness. I opened the fridge and took out a carton of milk and as I gulped it down, Rudolph meowed pleadingly. I poured some milk into his bowl, and he lapped away at it. A squawking caught my attention and I turned towards the bird on the window ledge; we locked eyes for a few seconds before it flew away. I was no animalogist, zookeeper, or whatever you call it, but from my basic knowledge, I knew a snow owl shouldn't be in these parts. The night wasn't even cold to begin with, but I didn't let myself think much of it.

I returned the milk to the fridge and as I turned away, I was surprised to find the snow owl I had seen outside right in front of me. It came to rest on the kitchen island and cocked its head to one side as if it was examining me. We stared at each other again, this time I was more shocked than fascinated. The owl's eyes glinted orange, and then it disappeared into thin air, leaving only a smoky orange cloud behind.

I closed the fridge and stroked the cat before going back upstairs to my room. My conclusion was that I was hallucinating because of how tired I was. With that thought, I fell asleep, hoping not to dream again.

The sun shone through the crack of the opened curtain, lighting up the room. I woke to the sound of scratching at my door. I tumbled out of bed and dawdled towards my closet. A pair of joggers and a navy-blue shirt caught my eye. I put them on. I combed my hair and as I opened the door, at my feet was K-9, the family dog. I got on my knees, and K-9 offered me a paw. I shook it and stroked him gently on his head as he liked this. K-9's tail wagged as he led me downstairs where I was welcomed by a table of sleepy and rather hungry-looking family members.

I sat at the table and greeted all the sleepy faces. Rudolph sprang onto the window ledge by the sink and meowed his greeting. Mum dashed downstairs and as if she was being chased. She quickly whipped up a large omelette for us to share. I walked over to the cupboard and grabbed the Coco Pops from the shelf. Mum passed me the milk while I chopped up a banana to add to my cereal as a finishing touch. I cut off a piece of the omelette and constructed a sandwich, which I ate at the table. I then made another sandwich for lunchtime and added a bottle of milk, an apple and an iced muffin, the usual packed lunch. I put it all into my bag and headed for the door.

I rode my bike to school as it was clear that no one was going to give me a ride. The wheels crunched against the gravel as I rode my bike to school. When I got to school, I secured my bike by locking it onto the bike rail and ran to try and get to class on time.

The machine which determined if I was late—a clock—rested on the archway just before maths class. It gonged just as I knocked on the classroom door, and the teacher let me in. I apologised for my tardiness, and the teacher pointed me to my seat. After I sat down, I received my first greeting of the day. "Wassup, bro," said Brutus Bentley, one of my jock friends and captain of the football team. The 'Gossip Girls' started talking or gossiping about whatever or whoever was the headline of the day. The nerds and the geeks were conversing in what seemed to morph into a loud debate. " That is enough," boomed Ms Merid turning away from us to start writing on the board. As soon as she had turned her back on us someone threw a rubber which hit the back of my head. Bentley got up and looked around, he saw

Jerry laughing and rushed towards him picked him up and held him up by a wall. " Don't you ever try to do that again," warned Bentley. No friend of Brutus' was messed with, especially a jock like me.

Ms Merid, our maths teacher, delivered her lecture, the usual Monday routine. She carried on about Einstein and how great he was and how great we could be if we put our minds to it. After that, I didn't really listen; I only caught the funny and most important parts of the lesson. I glanced out the window and foresaw the adventures I could have in the Cyprus woods, a perculiar set of woods which led from the school grounds to the neighbourhood where we lived.

It was a shortcut that people took when they were running late but I was careful not to use it because it a law put forth by the council not to set foot on the council's property.

Without even knowing it my mind had drifted into the woods which was normal. I could see trees and animals but one thing seemed out of place, the silhouette of a man who had a bright light shining out of his chest. I didn't know this man and I'm sure he didn't know me but I could sense that he was looking at me straight through my mind and at me and shockingly, it seemed so realistic. I had to figure out who that was.

"Mr Malcolm, am I disturbing you?" asked Ms Merid.

"No, you're not, Ms Merid please continue," I replied.

After about another eternity of twenty whole minutes, the lesson ended with a ring of the bell. Straight after the bell rang, I was called to the headmaster's office over the P.A system, the most embarrassing way. I was nervous, and so were my football teammates. A jock being called by the headmaster, or the 'Old Pig' as we called him because of his pig like body shape, was never a good sign.

Sweat beads formed on my brow my as I walked towards the office. My legs were like jelly and my hands trembled. At reception, I was given directions to the Old-Pig's office. I couldn't understand why they didn't just build his office next to reception. This just gave me more reason to be scared. The directions to his office echoed in my head: Go down the staff hallway, take a right turn, go up the stairs, and there will be an office labelled 'Headmasters House' it is on the left.

Chapter 2
HEADMASTER

I was right in front of the door, and I was terrified. Despite my terror, I grabbed the brass knocker and knocked on the varnished oak door, once, twice, thrice. Eventually, I heard a short buzz, and the door opened. About four metres from the door sat a rather short, stout, podgy, pug-faced man with silver- rimmed spectacles that encased his sullen grey eyes. He wore a crisp white shirt held together by an unmistakable H&Ms noir-tie that went below his buckle, covered by a premium sky-grey Giorgio Armani suit that just about fit him. The sun reflected off his pair of metallic-grey Jefferey West shoes. Mr Skipper definitely had a taste for fashion.

"Morning, s...sir," I stammered, fear evident in my voice. I looked around in his office. A bearskin hung over his desk. Behind him hung a pair of antlers which, from where I stood, made him look like he was half animal. The rest of the room was filled with fine paintings of forest animals. Through the shadows I could just make out a thin silhouette of a man on the floor beside his tiger-skin-carpet which was just a little bit out of place but vaguely familiar, the man from my daydream! But how did he make it to the floor of the headmaster? I wondered.

"Please take a seat. I have been expecting you," said the headmaster. His words brought me out of my trance, and I took my seat in front of him. I still felt scared but I was starting to feel more puzzled than anything else, was 'the Old Pig' working with the silhouette man? Or was he the silhouette?

"You have not been doing well in class. Your daydreaming and general absent-mindedness caught out by your teachers during lessons brought me to the conclusion that you are significantly distracted ." My heart was already on its way to my throat as he continued. "Many of your teachers have been complaining about your behavior as well as your grades. I have made the solemn decision that for now, your sporting activities shall be suspended."

I opened my mouth to speak, but I couldn't say anything. My sporting success was what landed me a scholarship at this school in the first place. My parents would be devastated.

"Not to worry, this does not affect your scholarship," said Mr Skipper.

I was relieved but still had my doubts. No sports meant that I wasn't a jock anymore. "But, sir—" I managed to say.

"My decision is final," the headmaster interrupted. "Pull up your grades, and straighten up your behavior. Or we may have to compromise," he concluded and we locked eyes as an orange glint flashed across his eyes.

Out of his office, I took into consideration the symbol on the floor, the silhouette of a man. First in my daydream then in Mr Skipper's office. Thinking about it, I could see a spherical light on his chest. The exact same person I had seen in my daydream in the woods. After just seeing it today I had a gut feeling I had seen it before.

Hidden somewhere under piles and piles of memories lay the recognition of this symbol. But I had a very odd feeling this memory wasn't mine.

I had only been gone for break-time and two other periods, but some people already knew what had happened. These people included 'The Gossip Girls', 'The Fortnite Squad', and Emelia, an ex-member of 'The Gossip Girls' and former head of the cheerleading squad. I knew it, it was obvious, Emelia had told everyone about my sports ban. She was by the reception when I went there, and she was waiting outside the headmaster's office when I walked out. Who else could it be? I just hoped that the rest of my squad hadn't been told yet. If they had, my life as a jock would be over.

The bell rang to signal the start of my sixth and last period, science. Mr Bismuth took register and then started talking about the importance of ancient artefacts and the science behind carbon dating as well as the tools used. But then he went off topic, blabbering about how he should be our history teacher. Next he explained how these artefacts were given to the kings of the area, and how it was believed that they gave them power. He told us this to give a bit of what he called 'background' to our learning.

We actually thought we weren't going to write anything until he gave us multiple formulae to write.

At the mention of ancient men, my head violently shook inside. It was as if I were trying hard to remember what I had only heard of today. I began to feel nauseous almost immediately after Mr Bismuth's off-topic speech. The floor danced in front of me. All my senses felt enhanced; I could hear everything from running water to the Mercedes Benz GLC 200 two and a quarter miles from here. Then it suddenly stopped, and I felt normal again until odium washed over me. I wondered if it was the disease of being a non-jock, but that was just unreasonable.

I ran up to our teacher and asked him for sickbay sheet (my passport to the sickbay during lessons). He looked up at me with his golden rimmed spectacles, the light shielding his eyes and he said,"Yes". This was very much unlike him but I didn't have the strength to determine other people's behaviour change. I grabbed the sheet and rushed out of the room.

I panted with my tongue stuck out, my feet hit the checkered floor heavily and it replied with a loud echo of my footsteps in a sequence. As I took the turn towards the sickbay corridor it was dark, darker than usual, there was no light, no light, no light at all.

Chapter 3
SHAPELESS

· · · · · · · · · · · · · · · · · ·

I was in the sickbay 'alley', the little hallway most commonly known as the Nerd Corner. This was where the nerds would be attended to after they were beaten to a metaphorical pulp. It was a one windowed, one curtained place which was usually lit up by the light from the one forever opened curtain. The nerds would come to this place to seek protection by the San sister who was quite a friendly lady.

In the alley I was tripped by something or someone and fell to the floor. I have to admit the people who knew I was off the team were treating me differently. People saying I should have never been on the team in the first place, that I was dragging the team down, that they were doing just fine without me, but it was all talk, no one had actually done anything or said anything to me.

"Come on man what did you do that for?" I mustered the strength to say. I didn't get an answer, all I got was darkness. As I tried to get up, a sudden pang of pain made me pin myself back to the floor. Just as well because at that moment, a shadowy figure swept over my body. Pure fear coursed through my body. Once again I was submerged in the feeling of odium, but this time it felt different, it felt welcomed.

From beneath me, a faint orange glow shone onto the checkered floor. I searched frantically for the source of light, only to realise that it was coming from me! I turned my hands so my palms faced me and I noticed a faint orange glow.

Those creatures from earlier, fixed their dark purple eyes on me. They approached me furiously. Almost instinctively, I raised my hands and the shadows shrunk back into the darkness. I kept my arms risen to keep the figures back. Hardly walking, I scrambled into the sickbay. The doctor opened the door and looked at me as if he knew me, then I collapsed into a world of my own.

I awoke to a voice that echoed around me. I could see some figures out of the corner of my eye. I was on a medical bed in the sick bay and the doctor was glowing orange as if he was giving off energy of his own. Sparks of orange energy danced around him and became dirty orange as they hit the ground. I blinked my eyes and for a few seconds, I could see normally, but it didn't last, soon I was back to the bright orange lens.

I looked around in deep concentration, trying to scan the room, moving my eyes but not my head. Everything else around the doctor glowed so faintly that it was imperceptible but he was the most brilliant light in the room, nothing else was really glowing, just him. I sat up but drew no attention to myself, then I looked at my watch it was five o'clock! I was 'asleep' for so long! How could I still be at school? My suspicion grew.

Slowly I reached for my duffel bag and slid off the bed in one fluid motion, walked to the door and opened it. I was always hearing stories of how crazy the doctor was, what he would do with people and animals. How he would entrust people with the responsibility of a 'magic' power or talk to animals and ask them for favours and expect them to comply. Complete and utter madness. I knew that he wanted something from me and I wasn't waiting to find out.

As soon as I stepped out of the room he shot a glare at me with his bloodshot eyes. I looked away and ran into the corridor. The darkness reminded me of the shadows I had encountered before. I wasn't ready to go back into the dark corridor, but anything was better than being in the same room as that maniacal doctor.

I ran into the corridor, everything still as luminous as it had been in the sickbay. The shadows returned as I ran down the hallway. I held my hands up but there was no light so they advanced towards me. I ran for what seemed like a lifetime through the classes and into the gym. I hid away in the gym bathroom. I could hardly see the shadowy figures, my sweat obscured my vision. I had to get out, crawling, I made my way into the corridor and stood up before tiptoeing, I hoped that the floor wouldn't make a noise but unfortunately the checkered floor replied to the steps from my trainers with a squeak which alerted the figures to where I was and I broke into a run. I was starting to seriously consider revisiting the maniacal doctor when I realised that I had trapped myself. Terror gripped me, I had run straight towards a wall and was at a dead end. The shadows hovered over me like vultures and almost instantly the feeling of odium swept over me again and I fell on all fours. My senses were enhanced, my sight level was lower, I could see my nose and the world around me looked brighter than the sun. I felt strong, my shoulders were tense and hunched, my tail swept the floor and I felt invincible.

I bared my razor sharp teeth. I felt the strength surge through my body, every muscle charged with energy waiting to pounce. My head was lowered as I cautiously studied my opposition. Then I noticed that the shadows were backing away. I looked at myself and I saw that my fur was radiating an orange light. I looked around one last time before jumping over the sea of shadows. Some shadows followed me. I instinctively bit them and they vanished into thin air.

I ran out the door, all the power and strength in my legs propelling me forward. Outside it was dark, so much time had passed whilst I was in hiding but none of that mattered to me anymore. I felt free, I felt a level of freedom and fearlessness I hadn't felt before and felt I could do anything.

The shadows reached for me but with my agility, speed and newly discovered glowing form I was unstoppable. Weaving through the trees that stood in front of me I could smell everything from the ladybird that rested on the newly emerged mushroom to the hyperactive rabbit that dashed into its rabbit hole to get away from the animal I had become. It appeared as a vivid image in my mind. I could smell their existence.

As soon as I lost the shadows I slowed down. I found myself in the Cyprus Woods. Slowly I drifted in and out of myself, out of the new form I had taken, it was like I was tired but forcing myself to stay awake. One moment I was in control, the next I was being controlled. I struggled with my subconscious but soon I was overwhelmed. I was now in the back seat of my conscious, the elucidation of myself.

I saw the ground rush up beneath me, as a puppet controlled by my subconscious. The sky showed us that it was dusk, we looked ahead. Suddenly an orange light from the sky shot down and caused a loud crash about 15 metres ahead. I ran towards it, now fully in control I skidded to a halt, my subconscious forced a smile across my face.

With my nose to the air, I sniffed around, a smell I had never smelt before filled my nostrils. I walked towards it, my head hung low, my shoulders swaying. Instead of a hole or crater in the ground a miniature hill had formed. Disoriented, I approached the makeshift staircase and worked my way up. On the summit rested a chest, I walked towards it and it opened as if I were a Bluetooth key. A bright light of orange colour shot into my face before dying down into the chest. I peered down into the box and discovered an orb and next to it rested a piece of ancient looking papyrus.

I sat down next to the chest and read what was written on the papyrus to myself, "Darkness and light, two shades, good and evil, two ways, the human race and the Mitigate, too soon."

Suddenly, the orb continuously changed shape, the piece of papyrus glowed gently. I lifted off the ground my paws dangling, a strong wind blew in the area and my fur shrank back slowly to show my human form. The orb shone its brilliant light from the chest. Trees bent towards me, grass leant inwards, branches hovered above the ground, all fallen objects rushed towards me, everything went orange, everything was so fast and lively. My body shuddered, I felt connected everything was in my command until it paused. Nothing moved at all, only I could. I could sense animals they were still alive but they had been paused.

Almost as suddenly as the pause had started, it stopped. Everything rewound, trees became straight again, grass fell back into place, branches gently dropped, twigs moved back to their stations. I fell from the sky, the wind blew and I fell and had the worst landing ever.

I ran my fingers across my body, hardly believing what had happened. I felt my head, face, feet and checked if I still had my duffel bag and surprisingly I did. I was shocked and amazed at how I had got here and done all this. I walked towards the chest and closed it, concealing the orange orb, then packed it into my bag.

The animals still lurked around. I flicked my wrist with an open palm and orange light illuminated the scene. Ecstatic and intrigued I approached them. Wolves, the connection towards them felt stronger than the others, that is when I knew what I had become, a wolf. They turned away from me and howled, running into the woods.

I looked at my watch, ten p.m. My Mum would be worried sick! I had power, the ability to influence others behaviour. I felt very powerful, but against an angry mothers tongue everyone is powerless.

I got home in thirty minutes, I climbed up the great Treehouse in our backyard, and slid into my room through the window. I put my bag down and tiptoed to my bed, the springs strained making a metallic bounce sound. The lights switched on and I knew that I was done for, busted.

My Mother glowered at me in a way that could have said I was the best player on the team and had just scored a goal from halfway or that I was the disappointment of the century. I looked up at her but only for a little while before hanging my head low and wiping my face. She came to sit next to me on my bed then she hugged me. She started talking about me being the big brother and setting an example as well as how she just wanted me safe before leaving me to sleep.

I slept knowing what I had experienced was incomprehensible to anyone else. I slept knowing only I could believe, and that the fairytale did not end here. This was only the beginning I could feel it, there was still more to come.

That night I had the dream, but it was different. It started the same: the unknown echoes followed by bizarre voices except that this time before I was swallowed by the non-certain shape I saw him, the silhouette of that man who I had first come across in my daydream. I called out to him but he just looked at me as if he were making a decision but I was still swallowed by that shape and I was trapped in that nothingness.

Chapter 4
BREACH

· · · · · · · · · · ·

*I*felt tired, as I woke to what I knew would be another day of ill-treatment. I was still light-headed from the day before, the room spun in circles around me as I waddled to the bathroom to complete my morning routine. I wore my normal outfit and looked at myself in the mirror and patted down the creases, combed my hair and packed my bag. The chest from last night felt warm, and from inside the contents glowed gently.

Just as I was about to go downstairs I heard scratching on my door. I knew that it was K-9 but as soon as he spoke in his bark I was uncertain. "Come on, hurry up it's almost breakfast," he barked. I stumbled a little in surprise, I knew that K-9 came by my door every morning, what I didn't know was if it was him. There was only one way to figure out the mystery, I slung my bag over both my shoulders, put on my shoes and opened the door.

At first I looked straight ahead, then at chest level and around the door, after a few seconds I looked down and saw K-9 sitting patiently, his tongue sticking out, as I stared at him my jaw dropped in awe. " Come on let's go," barked K-9 jumping around like a springbok and panting. I stood up straight, leaned back, yawned, stretched my neck, shook my head and straightened up and started walking down the stairs.

I went downstairs and only Dad was at the table so I got myself some Coco Pops cereal and went to sit down in the lounge to eat, I switched on the T.V and as normal it was on the news channel. I hadn't watched the news in a long time and so I decided to leave it on.

"The seven o'clock news, brought to you by Susie Carter," she said as she introduced herself. She mentioned a few things about global warming, made jokes, reducing carbon footprint in the city, the release of a new car from the well known Carre series, future technology and the one I was most attentive for, the mystery light of orange that shone through the woods by the local school. I put my cereal down and leant towards the T.V. " Some people believe that they have sighted an alien descending to Earth. Picture evidence shows you that the life form was orange. Trees are shown as if they are trying to reach the 'alien', scientists are looking for evidence at the scene of the event as well as in people's homes. Please do co-operate. Searches are to be carried out from seven thirty in the morning till sunset. This is Susie Carter from News Daily, thank you." As soon as she had finished I switched off the T.V and sank back into the sofa, wondering what I was going there was a knock at the door.

I ran up the stairs and when I was halfway up I called down to Dad," Some people are here to search the house."

"Okay I'll get the door," he replied hardly looking up from his morning paper. Rudolph and K-9 followed me into my room, thinking about what I could do with the orb. I took it out of my duffel bag, out of the chest and tried throwing it into the toilet but it didn't go anywhere, it was stuck to my hand. I could hear the stairs creaking they were close. Both my pets were asleep, so they weren't of any help. I was still in the bathroom when they knocked on my door. They asked me to open it but I remained silent. They then warned me of the consequences of my actions, that I may go to jail or juvie if I didn't cooperate. Only then did I realise the seriousness of the matter.

Without warning the search party kicked down the door and I found myself flushing the toilet and walking out the door. The people who formed the search party all wore black, they wore a black camouflage army uniform with bulletproof vests as well as dark tinted shades and earpiece to complete the mystery/action look.

Rudolph woke but went back to sleep, K-9 had his eyes open but was too busy sunbathing to take action. They began searching my room, I quickly kicked the chest under my bed but the orb was still very firmly attached to my right hand. They went through everything from top to bottom, stripped my clothes, looked through my 'toys' and general stuff. I was surprised to see them cleaning up after completely trashing my half trashed room but also relieved because first of all I didn't have to clean my room like what Mom had told me to do over a month ago and secondly because the search had been completed and I had not been caught, at least not for now.

Just as the search party was leaving one of the lady's got suspicious of why my hands were behind my back during the 'inspection '. She knew that it was definitely not for respectbecause the people of my generation were very low on the respect factor. " Is there something you would like to show us, mister ?" she cooed eyeing the hands behind my back. I shook my head, but showed them anyway, I felt my intestines dancing. I presented an open hand to them facing away but when I didn't hear a reaction I looked at my hand and saw a gecko, it was alive, I could feel it's heartbeat in my palm but it was seldom moving. " Oh," she said in more disappointment than I thought a person could express, " We will be on our way, sorry for disturbing you."

They went out through what splinters were left of the door and I was left by myself and my newly born gecko as well as Rudolph and K-9 of course. A few minutes after they had left my room to search the rest of the house the gecko flashed an orange light and was the orb again. I was fascinated. The orb had basically saved my life but that was too close, I couldn't take care of the orb anymore. I was somewhere between happiness and sadness, the only feeling clear was absolute confusion, I then made up my mind and threw the orb out the window. I didn't know what to do but it was over, all I could do was watch it fall to the ground. I wasn't going to even attempt to save it until I saw the lady who had the suspicion, it was about to hit her head and I was hoping that it may turn into an animal but in the heat of the moment I stretched my arm with an open palm and it came rushing back to me along with a few twigs and leaves. I had two solutions as to why the orb came back to me either because I had a strong connection with the orb or maybe that I had developed telekinesis and I was definitely going with telekinesis.

All these things almost took me off course for my main goal getting to school on time, I quickly packed my sandwich meals before jumping into the car with Dad for a ride to school.

Chapter 5
PREDATORS

· · · · · · · · · · · · · · · ·

*S*chool, now a playground for disaster. I parked my bike on the bike rail and walked into the main school building.

The school halls, the halls I used to run, if only I was like them, the bullies beating up people to do their homework. They had almost convinced me but I had values and I had to stick to them.

I still remember when we would walk down these halls, respected. No one would stand in our way. We were the predators and we were going to keep it that way. If only I were still one of them.

Overall jocks were very well known for their stupidity and their inhuman sporting ability. No one was as stupid as they were and no average 'Joe' had their sporting ability so it all cancelled out. What they lacked mentally they made up for physically. With everything there were exceptions and in this case it was Micheal Polo the one true all rounder. He was the football teams central defensive midfielder, skill, speed, game reading and agility were his top strengths and specialities. He was also in the regional swim team, played table tennis, rugby and club football. To add on to that he was near top for all of his subjects. Every teacher liked him and he had just been accepted into one of the best grammar schools in the country.

Then it happened, through the entrance door came the whole squad in a cloud of activity. Everyone made way for them and if they didn't comply they were rammed into the lockers, thrown to the ground or their lunch money was pinched, everyone moved, everyone except me.

They eventually got to where I was standing and then just stared at me with a cold stare that could freeze fire. It gave you the warning: caution, danger ahead, please take another route.

I stood there and looked at them as if they were meant to remember me, and they were. I had only been dropped from the team for about two weeks now. Everyone g around me looked at me, then reality kicked in, bringing the emotions with it too, embarrassment, loneliness, sadness and the burning sense of belonging had dampened out.

My mind was clear and I started again "Hi, my name is Malcolm, Marco Malcolm". They looked at me in disgust, everyone except for Micheal.

As the jocks saw I wasn't scared or even showing a sign of taking flight instead of fight they began to close in on me, I still didn't feel intimidated because I was taller than most of them. My hand formed a fist and my fist glowed gently which I hardly noticed but it seemed as if Micheal did because he looked a bit scared then composed himself and spoke up, " come on, its not worth it" he advised. They walked past me and all I got was an uncertain, frightened looking wink from Micheal.

After that I felt homeless. I had tried getting back to being a jock but my own 'teammates' didn't remember me. All hope was lost, I was to become a nerd now. I already had the Superman, Clark look going on, all that was left was a thousand page long physics book and making the library my playground. Eventually resulting in good marks and back on sport, then I would show them.

Lessons commenced as normal and straight after lunch I went to the football field. Coach 'try- hard' Johnson was already there, a sack of footballs sat by the bench. Coach Johnson was taking shots at goal post with no keeper, and missing. " Afternoon, sir," I said, taking him by surprise. He greeted me back and we started talking, I explained my situation and meet up with 'the team'. He listened as I knew he would and he reassured me. He asked me to take a shot, and I did, I scored top right corner and kept on scoring my football days were reanimated before my eyes, me dribbling through the middle and going out to the wing, my precise crosses to Bentley.

I reimagined myself running up and down the field waiting for the ball, waiting for my chance to shine. Running back for defence and running forward for attack to get a chance to score a goal.

With every shot I took I felt more and more happy, lighter as the heavy burden of sadness was slowly being lifted. In all my enjoyment and shot accuracy I forgot about my newly flowering ability. Then it happened, my hands glowed orange and an unusual amount of birds perched on nearby branches. Luckily Coach 'try-hard' was on his phone and didn't notice.

I quickly concluded the football session and ran away with my hands in my pockets. I ran into the hallway, I took a left turn then a right turn and turned in multiple other directions where I opened a wooden door with carvings of shapes and ancient animals. I pushed it and saw an orange swirl, I looked around through the swirl, this had to be the library.

It was just as well that I found as I needed to study anyway to get my grades up and this was the place.

The door was now opened and a swirl of orange light stood between me and the library. I could vaguely see the bookshelves and chairs. A bit scared I closed my eyes, stretched my arm and put it through the orange swirl. When I realised that my arm was fine, I stepped through the orange swirl and entered what I thought to be the library.

The floor was cold marble but the cloud soft carpets made it warm. The walls were made of bamboo sticks. A warm light of clear orange gave the room a warm chilled vibe. In the corners of the palace of warmth there were mattresses and bean bags, as well as heat massaging beds. This haven had another room extension called the snooze area just for good measure.

Studying was what I had come here for and so studying I would do. I took my books out of my bag and I had chosen a table at the back just in case anything happened. I arranged my study books on the desk in front of me. Every desk was accessorised with an Apple Mac Book Pro laptop. I switched it on and entered the world of studying.

Finally embracing my inner nerd, I concentrated harder and harder, the more information I got the harder I concentrated. Slowly I felt a warmth creep up my hand and into my palm. Suddenly a strong magnetic force ordered me to the doorway I had come through. Unwillingly I ran towards the doorway, arms outstretched and when I was by the door my legs shrank beneath me, I looked at my hands, orange, from my arms grew feathers and then wings. Instinctively I flapped my wings and I was out the hallway through the window and into the air.

Before I knew it I was out of the school and flying above the buildings and surprisingly towards my house. I could see my house though the small details were not so clear I could see everything else, K-9 sat outside on the doorstep, Rudolph was chasing his wind up mouse toy and Mom had just pulled into the driveway. The closer I got the more the small details were clearer. I could now see everything through my eagle eyes then I knew what I had become, an eagle.

My subconscious visited me again, forcing me to the ground. We flew through the Cyprus Woods where I had first witnessed power. I tried struggling with my subconscious before realising what it was doing, keeping me away from the poachers who hunted in this area. We rose, now closer to the house, I could finally see why I was here, the orb was glowing, and someone was trying to take it.

Chapter 6
MYSTERY

· · · · · · · · · ·

The cool air ruffled my feathers as I tucked my wings and plummeted towards my room's open window. The thrill of the cold air rushing past me gave me a feeling of ecstasy.

I flew through the window with folded wings before stretching my wings out to bring myself to a halt. The man who was trying to take the orb looked at me in awe and I could see his bloodshot red eyes that reminded me of the maniacal doctor. My subconscious took over and we both dived towards the orb. As soon as we made contact with it a flash of orange light filled the room and I was human again. The mystery man and I struggled for the orb but being bigger and more physically able bodied he managed to get the orb out of my hands. He ran towards the window ledge and briefly looked back before jumping out of the window and running into the woods I had come from.

As I saw him escape, a new feeling bubbled inside of me, the unforgettable feeling of defeat.

I still wondered why that man had stolen the orb from me. I kicked my shoes off and sat on the edge of my bed, my fingers interlocked. All I could think was why did I have this power? Who chose me? Why was it me? Did I always have this power? Then the most obvious tool came to my mind, the Internet.

My laptop was on my desk and I started typing: What does a magical sphere-shaped object that gives you the power to glow orange in colour, the power of telekinesis and the power to shape-shift mean? I hit the search button and my screen started making black and white pixels before it turned completely black, my hands glowed brighter than they ever had before, I tried clenching my fists but I couldn't the glow from my hands was too powerful, my screen now flashed black and white, everything except for the water in the room rose, orange web-like tethers shot from my hands and to the floating objects in the room, then I slowly rose off the ground with my hands held out, twitching, my legs together and my head facing upwards. I looked at my hands and the rest of my body in horror.

Somewhere in the room a growl of a voice had started and as it stopped everything dropped back into place, excluding me. Then I suddenly fell and landed flat on my back, on the floor, just as I thought it could not get any worse a lean man with long dreadlocks and an orange headband appeared by my window and said four words, "I'm your new teacher," before I fainted face flat on the floor.

* * *

Water entered my ears and nose before I woke. I sat up straight and pulled my knees to my body. I could see waves battling against each other, tossing and turning before crashing into each other and washing over the sand. I got up and looked around, judging by the lack of construction and abundance of waves my guess was that I was on an island. It was pretty big, about 55 miles long by my estimation. Without looking around I could sense animals and very faintly I could sense trees with fruit.

The inevitable squeaking of parrots brought my eyes to the sky and I stood to watch them fly over head. None of this looked familiar to me at all, apart from the coconut tree, the internationally recognised island mascot. Once again I had been brought somewhere against my will. I was infuriated! My hands started to glow but I quickly relaxed making them normal again.

Since I was here already I decided to explore the island, so I stood up dusted myself and shook off the sand and made my way to what I called 'The Coconut Tree Hill'. I walked until I was on the hill. There was no one there except for me and for a split second there was an unearthly silence.

Suddenly the same man I saw before I found myself in this place was in front of me. I looked at him and started asking him all the questions I had been asking myself in my room. He told me he could only answer one and he did. He told me that I was 'Semblance' and for the third time today I was transported against my will.

Chapter 7

TEACHER, TEACHER

· · · · · · · · · ·

I waddled to keep my balance as I materialised in the centre of my room. I stumbled backwards and almost fell out the window before my 'teacher' grabbed my shirt and pulled me back in. As soon as I was safe I held my hand back as if I had claws. My skin waved between fur and feathers as if I were to choose between the two. The fur coated me and the wolf advanced forward. He looked scared, I could sense his fear and I loved it, but it wasn't only him, there was someone else but that someone was him.

"Why are you bothering me ?" I questioned the 'teacher'. He slowly backed away from me, he looked terrified but I couldn't blame him I'd probably be scared of myself too. "Answer me," I growled, swiping a paw at him. Suddenly he disappeared in a wispy orange smoke cloud. I looked around only to see a snow owl swiftly glide round the room. Suddenly I understood, it made sense. " So you were the snow owl that day, as well as the headmaster on the day of my meeting," I said half in confusion and half in realisation. He nodded his snow coloured feathered head slowly in approval. " Now do you trust me ?" questioned my teacher still speaking telepathically. A wave of orange crossed his eyes before he turned human again. Just the same way as the first snow owl's eyes had glinted orange, just like him. It wasn't a dream he was the snow owl.

Now that I vaguely knew who he was as we kicked off to a conversation, this was his story: "I was about your age, maybe older, " he started. The way he said made him seem old but he didn't look that old, he didn't have any wrinkles to begin with." I had dedicated my life to exploration, I was in love with nature, but what really intrigued me were the animals. Billions of microorganisms, millions of animal species non of them being the same. No two were exactly the same. I loved conservation ever since I was young and my adoration carried me forward into being something I though I would never do. My love for animals made me one of the youngest recruits of a conservation company called S.P.A which stood for Specialised Protection Of Animals.

I became the youngest official British conservationist at 20, but I was ill- treated. I wasn't at all treated like the great cause I was made out to be. At work I was bullied by men much older than me. No one respected me," he chuckled sorrowfully.

"Every week the boss of the conservational branch I worked at would hold a meeting, here we would discuss our issues with the branch, put forward ideas for further development of the branch and debate the movement of the ongoing projects under the S.P.A. This week's meeting was held on a Friday as usual in the main conservation board room. The meeting progressed following the normal regime. At the end of the meeting instead of the routine talk a few agents were told to stay behind.

We were informed about a meteorite that had fallen in the Amazon jungle. Meteorologists had already been sent in to look for the meteorite that had hit but had mysteriously disappeared. Later on astronomers were informed and they believed that the key to finding the meteor was in the stars so they had worked out the coordinates of what was meant to be the meteor and sent in their men to find it. They came back claiming they couldn't find it and so more men were sent to just collect samples of the soil around the fallen meteorite scene. They revisited the site and did as they were told and tried to return but were trapped, their only escape was the helicopter they had come with but it had been destroyed and on it rested claw marks. They were stranded there for three days, we were told, and eventually rescued by a Red Cross vehicle as a checkup for all the men was issued. Whilst in the

THE LEGEND OF THE ORB

23

Red Cross facilities some of the men claimed to have seen a monster that always changed shape never staying the same, some complained of a bright light that was close but far that never let them rest and since the trauma of the no food or water had affected them this was no surprise to their Red Cross hosts, until they heard a few men speak of angels. At that point just to be safe they looked up the top protection of animal organisations and found S.P.A they dialled the number and they had contacted me. I picked up the phone and they told me everything that I have just told you. They think an animal made those scratch marks they just don't know what.

Everyone already knew what he was asking us to do. We all exchanged glances before he broke the icy tension with the obvious question of who wanted to go. Everyone faced the ground and I looked up. I answered him and told him that I would go. The faces of my workmates definitely reassured me, from this moment onwards I knew I was going to be respected by them and that was a start. I volunteered for the respect that it would give me not out of self - willingness. Of all the things in the world I knew I wasn't even close to being selfless, " he chattered.

"I stayed behind in the boardroom being told of the dangers and protection precautions I would need to take to be safe. As a member of the S.P.A I had captured herbivorous animals as well as the carnivorous beasts. Our job was to catch, save, keep, and rehabilitate into the wild but what he was telling me sounded way more serious, closer to an animals life, live to kill or live to get killed.

After a month of hardcore army-like training I was ready, camouflage uniform on, research pack on my back, and the spirit of a willing soldier installed to keep me going. I entered a helicopter to the Amazon jungle and skydived from it down into the all round, mostly green vegetational wonderland. The plants comforted my otherwise rough landing, as I scoured into the leafy bliss.

My nights were hot and my days even hotter, my diary was now half wet and I hadn't found anything but a stream were I slept my most sleepless nights. Never before had I seen an animal in this jungle let alone heard anything. My head was throbbing, my eyes couldn't shut and good food was wearing thin, soon enough I would be hunting. I had given up until a sudden ground shaking screech filled the sky and a glowing orange something that I suspected to be a bird flew past me and shot into the air, it cried out again and disappeared as if it had gone through the sky.

Suddenly my hopes were lifted and I rushed towards the place were the bird disappeared, a mirror like sky glistened before my eyes folding in and out of the mirror form, I touched the mirror like thing in front of me and it rippled revealing a cave that illuminated in many colours and it called me, drew me towards it, the mirror shattered reformed and solidified behind me. The cave whispered, it had a voice and it was directed to me, the sounds of liveliness were totally shut out of my ears all I could hear was the voice that beckoned me. I followed the light as wide eyed as a bug. No one was there but I felt welcomed and not by the empty voice that spoke from within the cave but people, people I could feel but were not there. A tunnel through the cave led me to a dead end. I was half out of my bug chasing light daze and heard the voice again this time it told me this, and I quote, 'Maybe you are worthy, you have reached the heart,' it said. I touched the wall in front of me and out of it came a concrete slab protruding through the wall I had thought was a dead end. The wall in front of me glowed, it changed colour from green, to sky blue, to green, to pink, to red, then to purple and then finally orange and then the colour didn't change. 'Someone does think you are worthy, time to see who,' the bodiless projection enquired. A ground tremor hit as the wall in front of me shook and opened like automatic doors. A loud grinding noise filled the air and dust obscured my view but as it settled my eyes set upon the most astonishing sight. Seven orbs stared at me, all of them being of different color. The orbs hovered above an erect log like stool with carvings of writing unknown to man. I wandered around the semicircle looking at each orb starting with the pink one.

As soon as I was close to it the rock above the orbs crumbled to form a face and with the voice of the bodiless projection it announced 'the first father'. Each orb changed form at will. 'You have been chosen,' muttered the obelisk in a soft but strong voice. 'Step forth into the Mitigate,' declared the stone face. I stepped into the circle that I thought to be the Mitigate and the stone face told me that the orange orb, the orb of Semblance had chosen me. Before I could touch it, it shot up into the heights of the cave before gently humming and flying straight into my chest. I felt alive in a new way, nothing could stand in my way.

I ran out of the cave and to a cliff I had never identified before, I was so ecstatic that I jumped of a cliff suddenly, my subconscious kicked in, my nose grew small and sharp, my legs shrunk to what felt like chicken legs, my eyes widened, my arms lengthened but my body was smaller, my long arms grew into wings and feathers covered my body. I was flying as a snow owl in the jungle through the mirror illusion then free as a bird and out of the jungle.

I had the power for five years and only found out that I didn't have the power a year ago. I could have been saving lives. But I didn't think to use for anything anyway. It's just I had become attached to the orb but all good things come to an end but I still did have some abilities like turning into the snow owl. My passion for animals was still in my heart. And one day I was drawn to your window as a snow owl, it wasn't my intention but the intention of the orb. I believe the orb sent me here, I believe it called me to you" he stated.

"I know what it feels like to be drawn to something you don't even know about, trust me I know but you gotta leave before my Mum gets here," I told him.

Before my newly fledged teacher left he taught me one more thing. He opened up my hand so that my palm faced upwards and told me to relax, to feel my connection to the orb and I closed my eyes my connection to nature, to imagine the world through an animals point of view and believe. I waited patiently, my connection getting greater with every second and out of the blue I felt the orb stick to my hand. I opened my eyes but saw that he was gone.

Maybe that teacher could actually teach, no matter our first encounter. Some things are better taught by a teacher than by yourself after all.

Chapter 8
SPARROW

· · · · · · · · · · · · · · ·

Ever since the talk with my teacher I felt as if we had come to an understanding. But what puzzled me the most was why he had posed as my headmaster and denied me of all my sporting activities. I knew that I wasn't really the brightest light in the room but he had no right to take all that I stood for away from me. I had to tell him and ask him why.

He always wore the Pirates of the Caribbean look of Jack Sparrow. His dreadlocks bounced to whatever he said and to every movement he made. Beads lay suspended in his head of hair, and an orange headband caressed his hair and he had the outfit to go with it. All he needed now was a pirate hat and crew. We were back on the beach where I had been unwillingly transported by my now official teacher.

The soft sand massaged my feet as I walked in it, the sun was high and the water shimmered. I found teacher seated cross- legged on the Coconut Tree Hill. As soon as I was next to him he turned to face me then suddenly extended his arms towards me and flapped them like wings, he flew backwards whilst I was covered in sand, and as if that wasn't enough someone tapped my shoulder and I looked into a sandy cloud which led to me continuously coughing and walking around in circles that mademe dizzy. This carried on for about thirty minutes and teacher wasn't even tired.

My official teacher looked at me and coughed up the words, 'again,' as he walked around me like a predator, the predator he was. He walked around me and disappeared. A strong pair of what I made out to be paws forced me down to stay on the ground. Then I saw it, a pair of fangs. A familiar voice entered my head, "fight back," it advised.

I closed my eyes and tried to change, nothing, my hands didn't even glow. Instead I pushed him off and ran away. "Change, " he urged me telepathically. " I can't, " I shouted back still being chased. Teacher stopped running after me and I stopped running. "Why are you doing this?" I questioned still panting. "Well if that is how you feel..." he had hardly finished his sentence when I found myself back in my room.

My 'teacher' faced the floor his long hair covered his face and I could not read the expression on his face. "Next training session at the same time tomorrow," he informed me in a rather solemn tone. Before abruptly leaving the room through the window. I was delighted that I had something to do in the afternoons but I certainly didn't approve of the method that was meant to teach me.

My daily excitement birthed from these afternoon training sessions that were held routinely at the strange beach which I had recently discovered how to get to myself through a secret passage that I had somehow made by reimagining the living things on the island, my teacher always found me there but I never told him how I would get there. After all the training I had done with him I still couldn't bring myself to say what I actually felt about this. I suspected teleportation to be one of the new powers granted to me by the Mitigate. Every day for half a month Sparrow repeated the same drill he had been doing since day one of training as I was starting to got annoyed I was about to break.

I had a training session and the everyday routine commenced, I was tired and annoyed, it was nothing to look forward to just a different form of torture. I was on the verge of breaking until I spoke up, "I give up," I told him straight. Everything around him froze, from the dust to the water and almost immediately he was by my side.

"You can't, " he said with a hint of heartbreak in his voice," the beings of chaos have already started to rise and you have met them, you haven't yet harnessed your power and ..."

"And what? " I said to him.

"Dissimilitude is awakening," he replied," Altruise shall soon follow and we will all fall to the hands of the Dissimilitude."

"What?" I started to say.

"Fine," he said, but there will be a time where the world will need you and I hope you will not turn down the chance to rise and become the hero I never was," and with that we were in my room, he sat on the window ledge head facing down while his dreadlocks shook in time to his head shaking in disappointment. He leaned back and flew out in bird form.

My head swum, the day had crashed, now my afternoon routine had been broken. All I had to look forward to now was school, nasty, very much ordinary school. No adventure boredom would now gnaw at me.

Chapter 9
CHANGES

· · · · · · · · · · ·

Days went by like trees in a car ride. It had been a week since my teacher had left me and flown into the unknown and I was a sitting duck.

My 'teacher' had told me of the bad that was coming to this world and that I was somehow stuck in the middle of it all. What my 'teacher' had told me sounded as if I was literally waiting for danger to come to me, and I was not one to wait for the opposition to come to me, I was going to find out about them before they could find out about me.

The library suddenly came to my mind. I packed my bag and took the orb with me. I told my Mum that I was going out and tried to summon the orange glow but it didn't work, I was losing my power. I tried to reach my subconscious but no sudden surge of power jolted my body, I was alone.

Downstairs the T.V was on and my Dad and little sister were watching. I sneaked past them and went outside. My wheels crunched as I rode my bike to school and the gravel coughed. Then it all seemed familiar, history repeating itself.

I secured my bicycle in the bike rail before speed walking towards the football field. I found Coach Johnson on the field as normal except that he wasn't kicking a ball, he was talking to a rather shady looking man who wore a top hat, a black leather trench coat and shades at the edge of the Woods Of Cyprus. As he wasn't paying attention to me I easily sneaked past him but I still had my suspicions.

The hallway door from the football field was held open by a metal hook on each one of the doors. I thrust my hands into my pockets before taking many turns hoping to end up in the mysterious library.

The welcoming carvings of unknown animals and questionable shapes welcomed me once again to what I knew to be the palace of warmth.

The odd, library was still a familiar point to me, except for the extra rows of books that rested, centralized in the room. Many people bustled hurriedly around the library, bringing a sense of discomfort to the place. It was not as warm as it used to be. The mountains of beanbags had been subtracted to a rubble, the once soft carpet now felt like I was walking on a floor of nails, the clear orange light now looked as if it shone through a dirty light bulb, and the 'snooze pods ' were now replaced by stations that looked like playing a car game in an arcade but more like a control spaceship from home thing.

Rather panicky voices rang through out the room. I had never been quite a social person but with the drastic change in scenery, I had to question someone. Something told me that this wasn't a library. And if it was something was definitely happening something very bad.

My knees had 'dents' in them after I stood up from what felt like a nail coated carpet. I had crawled to get past the crowd of people partly because I thought it was a clever idea and partly because I thought that I would change into an animal.

I was surprised no one had noticed me as I wasn't as stealthy as anyone in class or anywhere for that matter, but I believe that it was with my animal instincts that I was able to get past the crowd of people.

Socialising definitely wasn't my strong suit, I sought for a life of adventure, of liveliness and above all action, I would have to work this out by myself.

Chapter 10
DARKNESS

· · · · · · · · · · · · · · ·

The excitement of it all was so overwhelming that it reminded me of my other persona, my second personality.

I was now at the back of the so-called 'library ' and was now on my way towards the 'snooze pods' before a book on the bookshelf closest to the 'snooze pods' area caught my attention. It was a smooth brown leather-cover book with an Aztec looking symbol, in the middle of the front cover, it felt like it was calling me like an invisible force was pulling me towards it I felt as if I were a big being drawn to light and as soon as I touched it, it glowed a faint orange giving me a sliver of hope before the room went dark and the ground beneath me crumbled and opened up.

The mouth of the darkness swallowed me as I fell to what I knew would be my death, I knew that nothing could save me now, luckily I had the book to keep me company, not that it could talk or anything, after all you can't read in the dark so I was as good as on my own. My shapeshifting persona had deserted me, the comforting glow had darkened to nothingness and worst of all I had lost what my teacher had told me about the most, the power I had once possessed. I had always thought that when someone was about to die their life would flash before their eyes, but not for me, I simply remembered everything I had done wrong since I started shapeshifting and I was still falling.

When I had lost all hope the warming smooth brown leather cover book's Aztec symbol glowed and the books now golden turned themselves faintly glowing a clear yellow light. This book was more than what it appeared to be, I could faintly sense a person but I knew it couldn't be a person in a book, it was something, and it was going to help me hopefully.

I had had powers for two months, I had suddenly started shapeshifting after an encounter with the beings of chaos, found an orange orb that strengthened my power, I met a mystery man who miraculously became my teacher, I battled a man who tried to take the orb from me and found a library that is only visible to me that I was now falling through.

The book shone enough for me to see the bottom of my fall, on the floor, spikes of what looked like diamonds that were never a certain shape glowed seven colours alternating between each colour. Red, orange, ice blue, green, pink, purple and colourless if that was even a colour.

The book slipped out of my hands and fell in the direction of the multicolour spikes, the light from the book slowly turned from yellow to orange. Then I finally knew where my power was, in the book! I was getting closer and closer to the spikes, my endless fall was coming to an end. I rummaged through my memory to try and find a way to get the book. I thought back to my training, to the rough conditions of what I thought of as abuse and finally the answer was found, I concentrated and connected myself to everything, all life and shapes were in my control. I then held out my hand and waited, in the distance I could see a faint glow, it was above me, in a few seconds I felt something in my hand, it was spherical and definitely the orb. I felt like Thor from Marvel because I knew this was the orb.

As soon as it was in my hand I pointed it towards the book and the book flew to me like there was an amplified magnetic force pulling the book towards the orb, I pushed the orb into the book, the orb and the book fused and the orb shone in brilliant light, the book was nowhere to be seen, all that was left of the book was these words in a cloud of orange:' The Book Of Life.'

Now I was getting close to the end of my fall I thought of a bird to turn into and concentrated. From my body grew feathers, my arms grew weaker and longer, more feathers grew on my arms, my nose and mouth merged together to form a beak, my body shrunk and my feet turned to tough skin and talons, my eyes grew bigger and the darkness around me lit up. The reflection on the orb showed me that I was a snow owl and suddenly the orb rocketed into my chest and I gently glowed orange in my bird form. A few centimetres from the spikes I flapped my wings and soon found myself out of the hole that had been made.

Back on the surface the library looked as if it had been a wheat field that had been hit by winter and left completely barren. The carpets had been torn to threads, the bookshelves had been smashed to smithereens, the room was very cold and to my despair there was no light, I was the only light in the room and all eyes were on me.

Chapter 11
SEMBLANCE

· ·

It was early evening. The library looked as if it was being evacuated. I made no sound but all the eyes in the room rested on me, it was silent for a moment before a low raspy growling chorus broke it,"we are Phantom Nebulo, the first soldiers to join Dissimilitude's army, we are chaos." The Phantom Nebula charged at me but with my natural athletic capability and enhanced skills I had dodged all their attacks. I landed and changed back into a human and with a new found confidence I replied with a rather deep voice that wasn't mine," and I am Semblance."

The people of the library didn't stick around to watch the battle they saw this as an opportunity to flee and so they did. They all gathered by a wall and chanted in a language that was not of this world until a brilliant white light shone through the wall. It was a portal and all of the library people jumped into it and through the wall to wherever they were going.

While I was busy watching them escape, one of the dark shapeless figures attacked me. I was on the floor and they were piling on top of me, I struggled and struggled trying to get out of the doggie pile that they had created. I reached a state of true panic, I was screaming hoping that someone may come to my aid, then I realised that I was alone, no one could save me except for myself. I concentrated and slowly I began to change form. My shoulders grew, they were hunched and tense, my head stretched to form a snout and a mouth that was filled with razor sharp teeth, I grew a bushy tail, claws grew out of my hands that soon turned into paws, the darkness became as clear as day and finally a coat of grey fur sprouted on my body and with a burst of strength I threw the beings of chaos off my back, my razor sharp teeth were bared, my ears slick back I was ready for the next attack, I was ready to fight.

The Phantom Nebula looked a lot like Wild-mutt from Ben 10 except that they were completely black, had purple eyes and no Ben 10 watch on their arm and they weren't friendly at all, they literally were chaos. They reeked of something more rotten than eggs and they seemed to have their own language because as they attacked me they would whisper a throat scratching phrase of coordinated coughs and more would come to assist them. The gills were what kept the creature alive is what I thought, I had even tried to cover them but nothing happened. It just kept on breathing in the same way as it had been. As I said before these creatures were just pure chaos.

My fangs hung out of my mouth and I faced the enemy, my front legs were outstretched, my back legs were ready to rocket forward, my fangs bared ready to hit whatever got into my way. To my delight I found myself running towards the exit, my subconscious had returned.

We were by the door. My subconscious and I were working together to make it out of here. I wanted to run away in truth I was terrified but if I were to let these creatures run free who knows what damage they would cause. I had to stay and fight off these creatures, the words of my former teacher echoed in my head: 'there will be a time where the world will need you and I hope you will not turn down the chance to rise and become the hero I never was'. This was the time to show that I was a hero, after all fear is just another reason to keep trying.

I turned back into a human from my wolf form and peeked through the door, the beings of chaos seemed to be increasing. I looked around and found a purple-black portal that was transporting them into the room. I knew what I had to do. I looked around again and saw the least expected thing, a key, then it became obvious to me, I had to lock them in the library.

My entrance had to be discreet, my subconscious took over. I felt myself shrink to what felt like nothing. As I shrunk hair grew all over my body, my limbs shrunk to the size of needles, I grew another pair of what I thought to be either legs or arms, my back arched and from my back sprouted wings, my mouth looked like a chute, all my hair was black, suddenly my vision split in front of me I could see multiple images at once from the puzzled Phantom Nebulo to the trashed library and I started to wonder if some of my power came from here, I stumbled before regaining my balance and I could hardly see. The vision of this animal and of my normal human vision made it seem as if I were looking through a red lens and it was then that I realized what I had become, I was a fly. I zipped past the creatures and found myself in the 'snooze pods' area, the key was only a few centimetres away and as soon as I landed on it and started the reverse process to become human again, but as soon as I did the other beings in the room had found me. I slipped the key into my pocket and made a run for it. I thought that I was going to get caught but instinctively I waved my hand and a bookshelf shielded me from the creatures in the room. I ran faster and faster and found myself changing, I grew hooves and my backside stretched, my hair was a chestnut brown, I had white socks, I grew a tail of silky black hair, my head grew and my eyes grew bigger and moved to the sides of my head an involuntary neigh confirmed I was a horse. I broke into a gallop speeding through the library, the creatures were gaining on me but after a couple of vigorous shakes of my head the bookshelves came to my assistance and they were left behind.

Soon I was by the door and I couldn't figure out which symbol the key was meant to go to. The creatures I had left in the library rushed towards me with the certain intention to injure me and I closed my eyes to try and concentrate but with a little help from my subconscious I locked the door.

The Phantom Nebula tried to break out of the prison I had made for them but they were trapped. I had done my job. The first step to being a hero. I knew that this wasn't the end. I walked back home even though I had my bike. I was exhausted, there was no other way to get home. I could still see Coach Johnson out on the football field, he hadn't noticed me but I saw him walk away from the shady man in black who wore the trench coat that swept the grass. He looked sad as if something bad was going to happen, I had a growing suspicion but I was to tired to do anything about it.

When I got home I went straight to my room, of course my parents didn't even suspect anything, it wasn't even that late anyway. My curfew was only at eight o'clock and right now it was seven o'clock. I just skipped supper and went straight to my room. I reflected on my day, my plan was not the wisest, the Phantom Nebula may be able to breakout of the library at anytime but I was hoping that the 'mystical' bonds that kept the library hidden might keep the beings of chaos at bay. I might have succeeded for now but no one would be safe from now on. I would have to protect these people it was now my duty, the duty of the one who possesses the orb, the duty of Semblance.

I went to sleep straight away, my bed looked more welcoming than a charge of angry Phantom Nebulo. As soon as my head hit my pillow I was asleep. The dream started in the same way all the time first were the unknown echoes followed by the bizarre voices but this time I wasn't swallowed by the mystery shape instead the shape gave me way for me to get past it. When I walked past the shape I saw the man, he wasn't a silhouette anymore, he radiated orange he held his hand out to me and as I reached out to take his hand my hand dissolved and I fell back into a hole like the one in the library except that this time at the bottom waited a dragon. The man looked down into the hole I was falling into. His face read an expression of laughter and happiness but his tears told a story of sorrow and sympathy. The dragon was dirty gold in colour, it's fangs hung out of its mouth, it breathed smoke out of its nostrils and waited, waited for me to fall right into its 'hands'.

I woke up in an instant and looked at my watch, it was 3 a.m. I drank some water out of a bottle that I had put by my bedside. As I put it down I sensed something you the window, my skin wavered between fur and feathers and I chose fur. I looked at the window and there sat the dragon from my dreams. My subconscious was awake and it told me that this was Gallus, Dissimilitude's first in command. We locked eyes and then I saw something very odd sympathy as well as a person, my teacher.

Printed in the United States
By Bookmasters